# Squawk to the Moon, Little Goose

# Squawk to the Moon, Little Goose

○

## Edna Mitchell Preston

### *Illustrated by Barbara Cooney*

THE VIKING PRESS    NEW YORK

○

*First Edition.*
Copyright © 1974 by Edna Mitchell Preston. Illustrations copyright © 1974 by Barbara Cooney Porter.
All rights reserved. First published in 1974 by The Viking Press, Inc. 625 Madison Avenue, New York, N.Y. 10022.
Published simultaneously in Canada by The Macmillan Company of Canada Limited. Printed in U.S.A.
SBN 670-66609-2. Library of Congress catalog card number: 72-91349. Pic Bk.
1  2  3  4  5  78  77  76  75  74

Mrs. Goose put all her goslings to bed.
She said, "I am going next door
                    to visit Mrs. Hen.
                    Be good goslings.
                    Don't get out of bed.
                    Go to sleep."
And out she went.

Good's good and bad's bad.
Out of bed jumped Little Goose
    Across the floor
    Out the door
    Down the hill to the pond.

Splash! Up tail
  Down tail
  Dive and roll over.

A big golden moon sailed high
 over Little Goose's head.
Ho! A white fox was sneaking up
 on the moon.

Little Goose said, "Look out!"
But the moon did not hear.
Closer, closer crept the fox.
And then ho! the moon was gone.

Little Goose said, "Good's good and bad's bad.
        The fox has swallowed the moon.
        I must go and tell the farmer."

Away from the pond
Across the meadow
Down the lane to the farmhouse.

*Squawk! Squawk!*

The farmer said, "Confound it!
                What is the matter?"

He stepped outside to the lawn in his nightshirt.

He said, "It is you, is it, Little Goose?
            What is on your mind
                that you wake up a man
                in the middle of the night?"

Little Goose said, "Farmer, Farmer!
                    The fox has swallowed the moon."

The farmer said, "Ho!
                    Then what is that
                      up there in the sky?"

It was the moon, big and round and golden.

The farmer said, "Go to bed, Little Goose.
                    Don't bother me
                      with any more nonsense."

He stepped inside and shut the door.

Little Goose waddled away
   with her head hanging low for shame.

   Up the lane
   Across the meadow
   Back to the pond
   With her head hanging low for shame
   And she never once looked at the sky.

Ho! What was this she saw?

The moon was in the pond,
   caught in the weeds
   shining up through the water.

Little Goose said, "Good's good and bad's bad.
                  The moon has fallen into the pond.
                  I must go and tell the farmer."

   Away from the pond
   Across the meadow
   Down the lane to the farmhouse.

   *Squawk! Squawk!*

The farmer said, "Confound it!
                    Can't a man get any sleep?"

He stepped outside to the lawn.

He said, "You again, Little Goose?
            What now?"

Little Goose said, "Farmer! Farmer!
                    The moon has fallen into the pond."

The farmer said, "Ho!
                    Then what is that
                    up there in the sky?"

It was the moon, big and round and golden.

The farmer said, "Go to bed, Little Goose.
                    Don't bother me again
                    with nonsense."

Little Goose waddled away
    with her head held back
    so that she could watch the moon.

    Up the lane
    Across the meadow
    Back to the pond
    With her head held back,
    Keeping her eye on the moon.

HO! That is how it happened
    that the fox caught her.

    SQUAWK! SQUAWK!

Across the meadow
and down the lane
in the farmhouse
the farmer in his bed woke up again
and heard,

SQUAWK! SQUAWK!

The farmer said, "No! No!
            Not again!
            I won't get out of bed
                for any more nonsense!"
And he rolled over and went to sleep.

SQUAWK! SQUAWK!

There was no one to hear her,
    no one to come and help her.

The fox said, "Now I am going to eat you."

Little Goose said, "Please don't eat me.
     I will give you —
     I will give you —"

The fox said, "A fat hen to eat?"

Little Goose said, "No! No!"

The fox said, "A tasty duck to eat?"

Little Goose said, "No! No!"

The fox said, "Then I will eat you."

Ho! What was that in the pond?

Little Goose said, "I will give you —
     I will give you —
      a cheese as big as the moon!"

The fox said, "Little Goose,
            you can't fool me.
         You have no cheese."

Little Goose said, "Ho!
               Then what is that
                  down there in the pond
                  caught in the weeds
                  big and round and golden?"

The fox said, "A cheese as big as the moon!
            I will eat it up."

Splash! The fox was in the pond
and Little Goose was running
running straight home.

Good's good and bad's bad.
Mrs. Goose spanked her
and gave her a scolding.

Mrs. Goose said, "Hop into bed.
                I will tuck you in.
                Be my good little goose now."

Little Goose said, "I will."

E                              9848

Preston
Squawk to the
moon, Little Goose

**Date Due**

| JUN. 8 1977 | | 59 OCT 1 9 1995 | |
| AUG. 1 9 1978 | | 9 FEB 1 9 1998 | |
| MAY 2 3 1981 | | 386 JUN 1 1 1998 | |
| AUG. 5 1981 | | | |
| APR 1 1 1987 | | | |
| 12 4 AUG 1991 26 | | | |
| 622 | | | |
| 28 JUN 1995 | | | |